# William Bee's
# Wonderful World of
# Tractors and Farm Machines

| PAVILION |

First published in the United Kingdom in 2018 by
Pavilion Children's Books,
43 Great Ormond Street, London WC1N 3HZ

An imprint of Pavilion Books Limited.

Publisher and Editor: Neil Dunnicliffe
Art Director and Designer: Lee-May Lim
William Bee's Agent: Jodie Hodges
Farming consultants: Simon and Sarah Righton,
Old Farm, Dorn, Gloucestershire, England

ISBN: 9781843653547

A CIP catalogue record for this book is available
from the British Library.

10 9 8 7 6 5 4 3 2 1

Printed by Toppan Leefung Printing Ltd, China
Reproduction by Tag Publishing, UK

# William Bee's Wonderful World of Tractors and Farm Machines

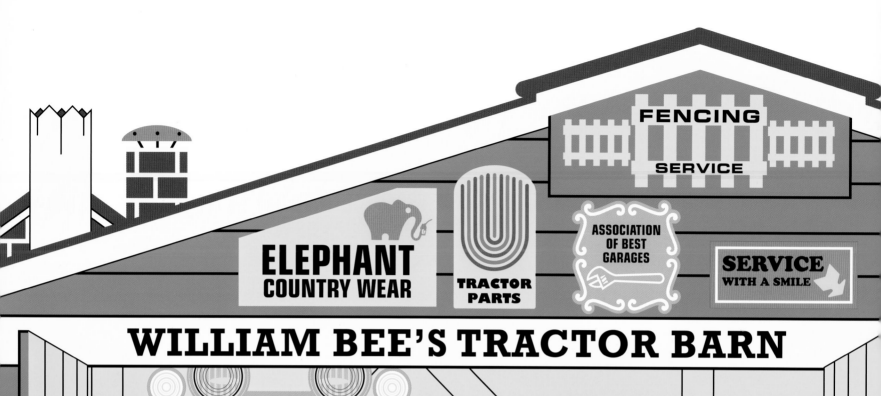

# WILLIAM BEE'S TRACTOR BARN

Hello. I am William Bee, and this is my Wonderful World of Tractors and Farm Machines.

Tractors and farm machines help farmers grow most of the food we eat. Potatoes and sugar and wheat and peas and carrots and apples and strawberries and... well you get the idea.

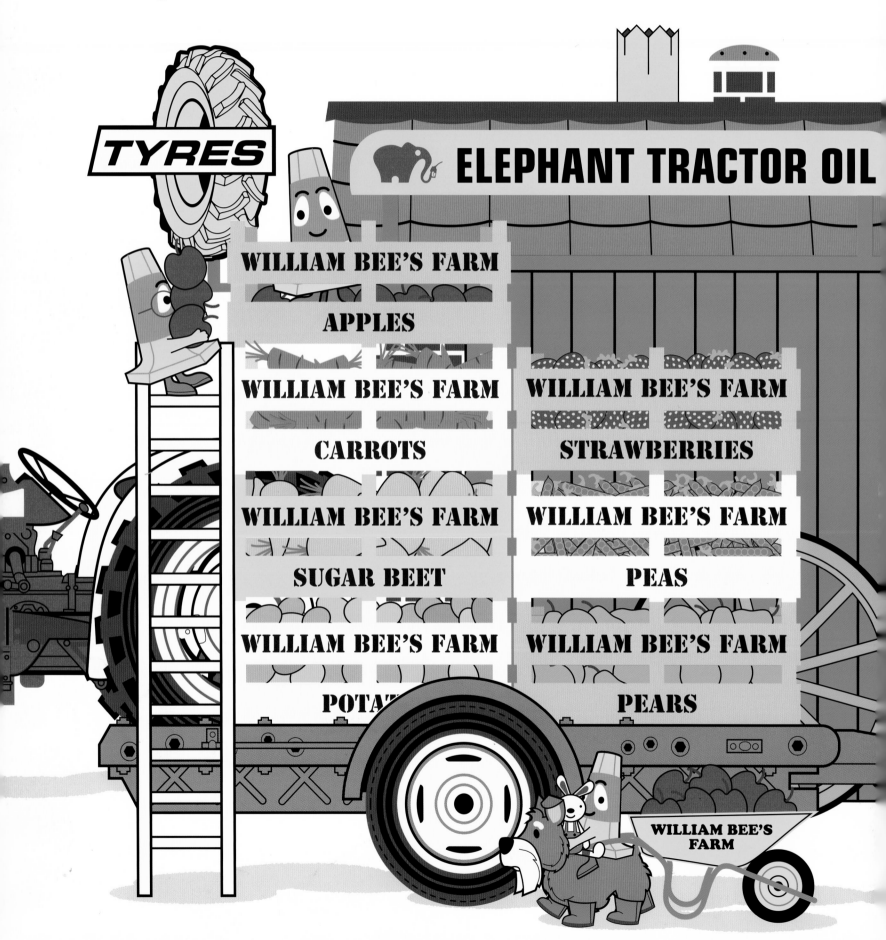

TYRES

ELEPHANT TRACTOR OIL

WILLIAM BEE'S FARM

APPLES

WILLIAM BEE'S FARM

CARROTS

WILLIAM BEE'S FARM

STRAWBERRIES

WILLIAM BEE'S FARM

SUGAR BEET

WILLIAM BEE'S FARM

PEAS

WILLIAM BEE'S FARM

POTAT

WILLIAM BEE'S FARM

PEARS

WILLIAM BEE'S FARM

If it wasn't for farmers there wouldn't be any bread, or pasta, or chips, or sweets, or cakes, or cereals, or jam or... anything much to eat at all!

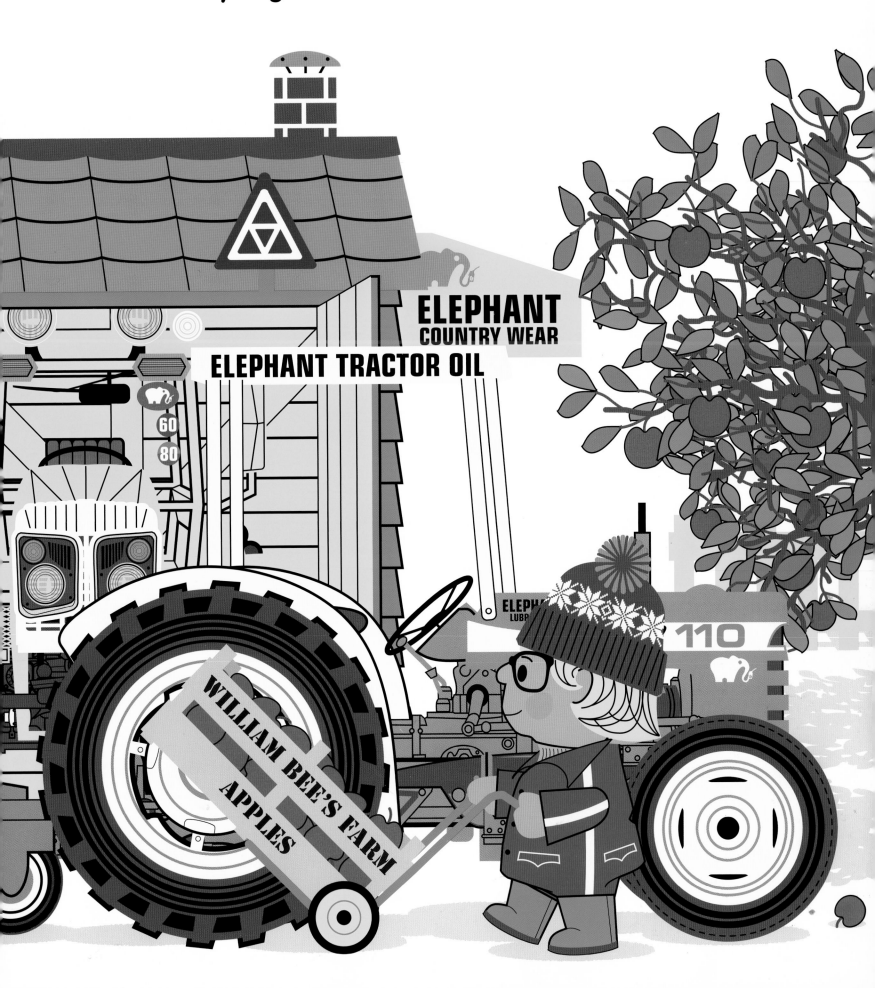

# Tractors are the most useful of farm machines.

They can be very small and thin – like this one.
It can get between apple, pear and plum trees
without knocking the fruit off all the branches.

WILLIAM BEE'S FARM

APPLES

Tractors can be very, very big –
like this one. It can cover hectare
after hectare – if you have a very,
very big farm.

HARVESTER
GREASE

TRACTOR
GREASE

It's wider than most tractors are long...

TRACTOR GREASE          HARVESTER GREASE

...even one as long as this.

It has four great big wheels and two great big engines – like two tractors joined together – which makes it very powerful and perfect for pulling the heaviest machinery through the thickest mud.

It's all the pulling and pushing and carrying
and lifting that makes tractors so useful.

They are useful because of *what* they can pull
– like this plough.

Ploughs prepare the ground for planting.
They turn the soil upside down
(and downside up), burying all the weeds.

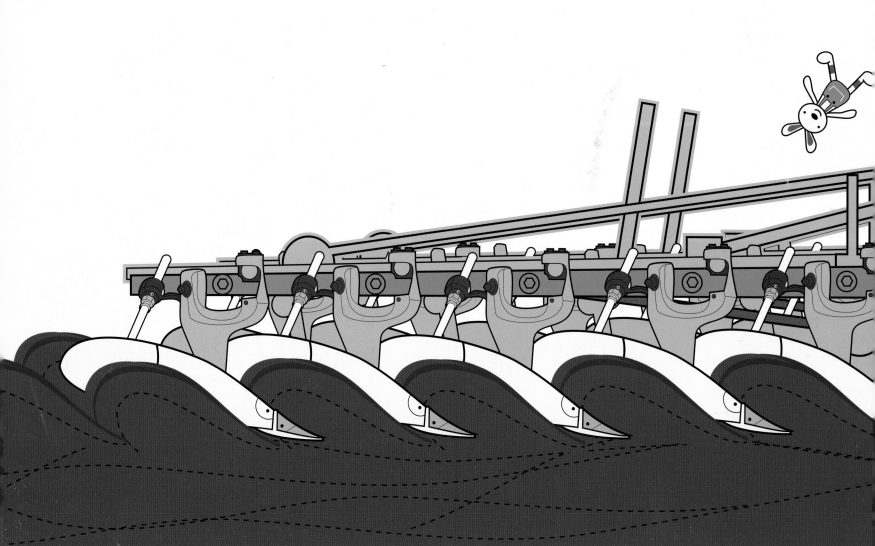

Tractors are useful for what they can push –
like this great big pile of smelly manure.

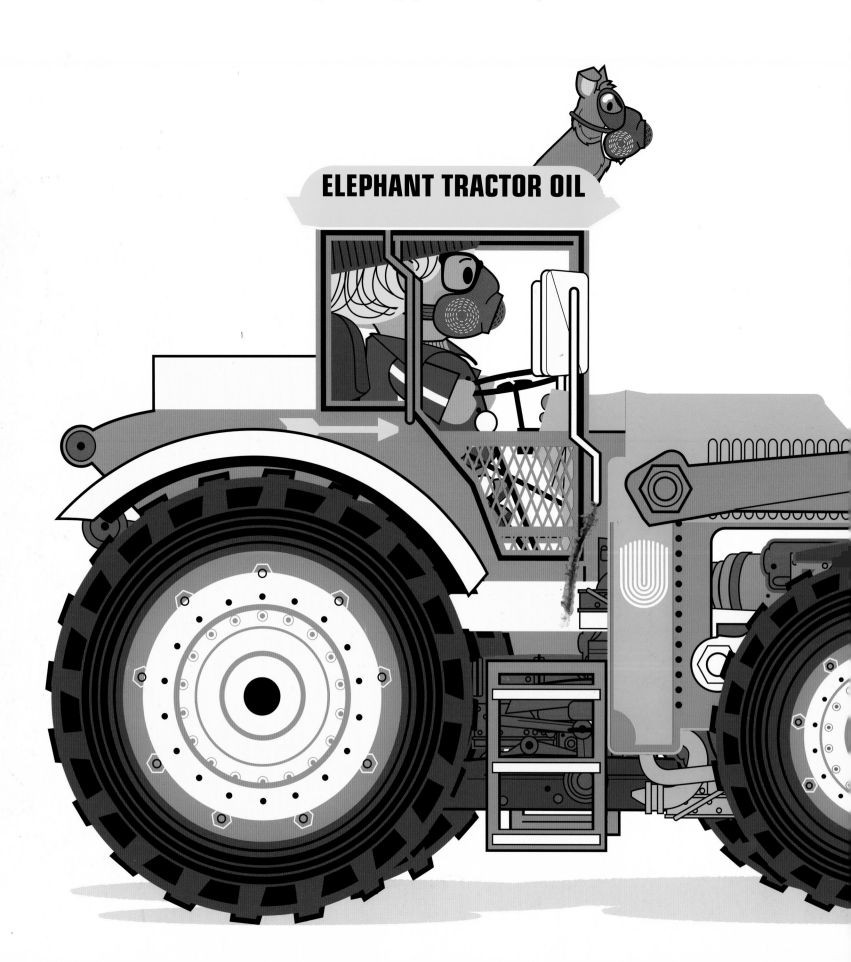

ELEPHANT TRACTOR OIL

It gets spread over the upside-down soil and adds lots of natural (and smelly) goodness to help the crops grow.

Tractors are useful for what they can pick up –
like these three great big tree trunks.
They weigh as much as another tractor.

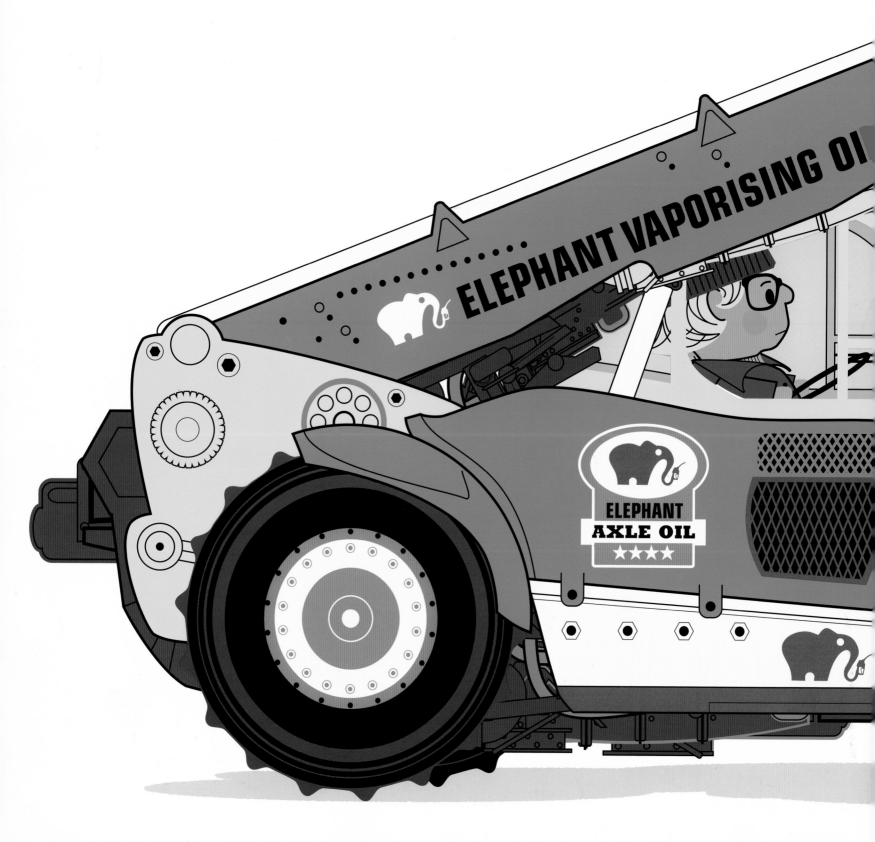

Tractors are useful for what they can scoop up – like these potatoes.

They are shaken about to get rid of the dirt and then loaded into this wagon.

Tractors are useful for what they can carry
– like this tank full of fertiliser.

It gets sprayed onto the crops,
to help them grow bigger and healthier.

And tractors are useful for where they can go – which is pretty much anywhere.

Some tractors have big wheels for going over hard, dry, bumpy ground.

And some tractors have tracks – just like tanks and bulldozers – for wet, soft, muddy ground.

Like this one.

Not that I have any intention of proving it – mine is brand new and I don't want to get it dirty.

Farms and farmers have been around a lot longer than tractors. So what did they use before? Cows. Like Daisy and Buttercup.

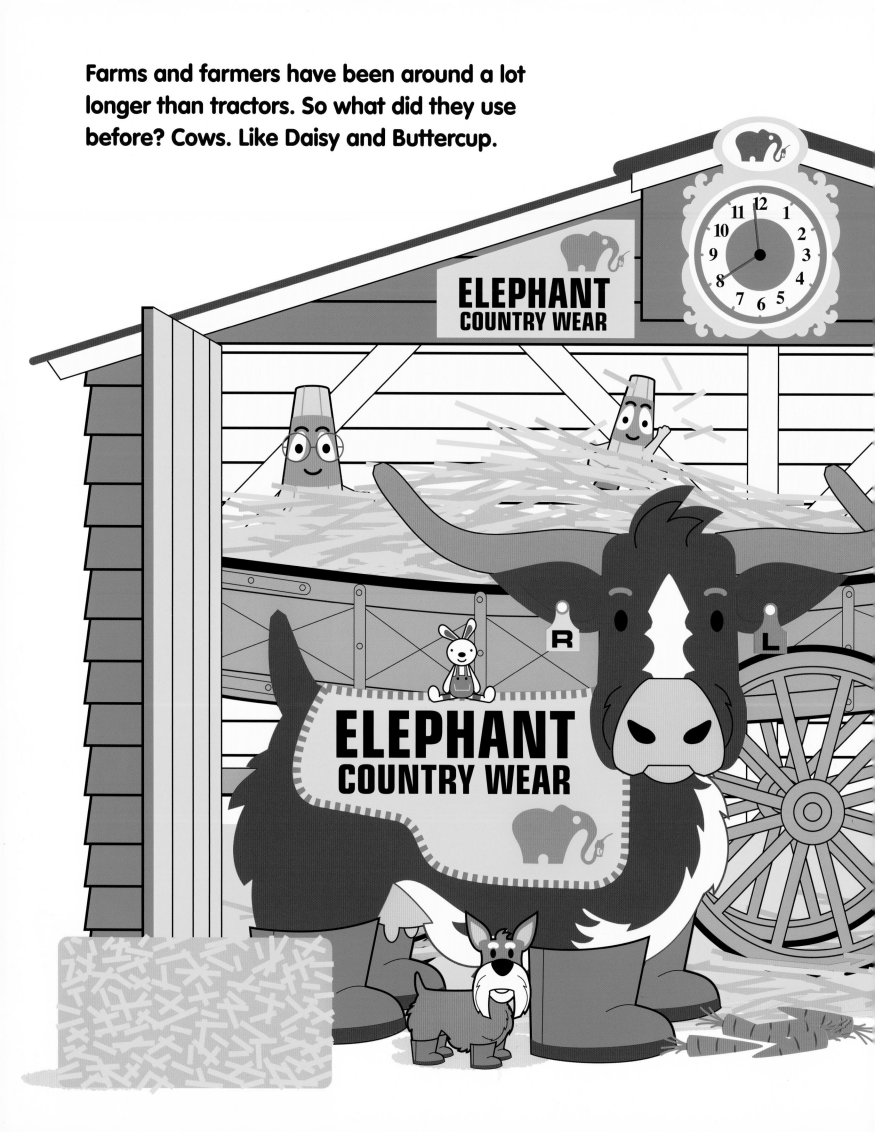

Or maybe a big horse, like Brian.
They could pull the ploughs across the fields,
or the wagons full of crops.

The first tractors were steam engines, powered by coal. Like modern tractors they were used to power farm machines that didn't have engines of their own.

Like this great big wooden threshing machine. Because threshing machines do not have an engine, the wheat has to be cut by hand and dropped into the top.

Then it separates the bit at the top of the wheat – the grain – which makes our bread and cereal, and the straw which the likes of Daisy, Buttercup and Brian sleep on.

Today's threshing machine is called a combine harvester.

It does what the old one did, but because it has an engine it can go along cutting (harvesting) the wheat itself.

Then it sorts the grain
from the straw,
like the old threshing
machine did.

The combine harvester drops Daisy, Buttercup and Brian's bedding in a neat line along the field. Then we use this – my self-propelling fully-automated straw baler.

It gathers up all the loose straw, squashes it tightly together and drops it out of the back.

Hey presto! Straw bales!

There is another machine on the farm that is not powered by an engine, or even by Daisy or Buttercup or Brian.

You may not even know it is a machine at all...

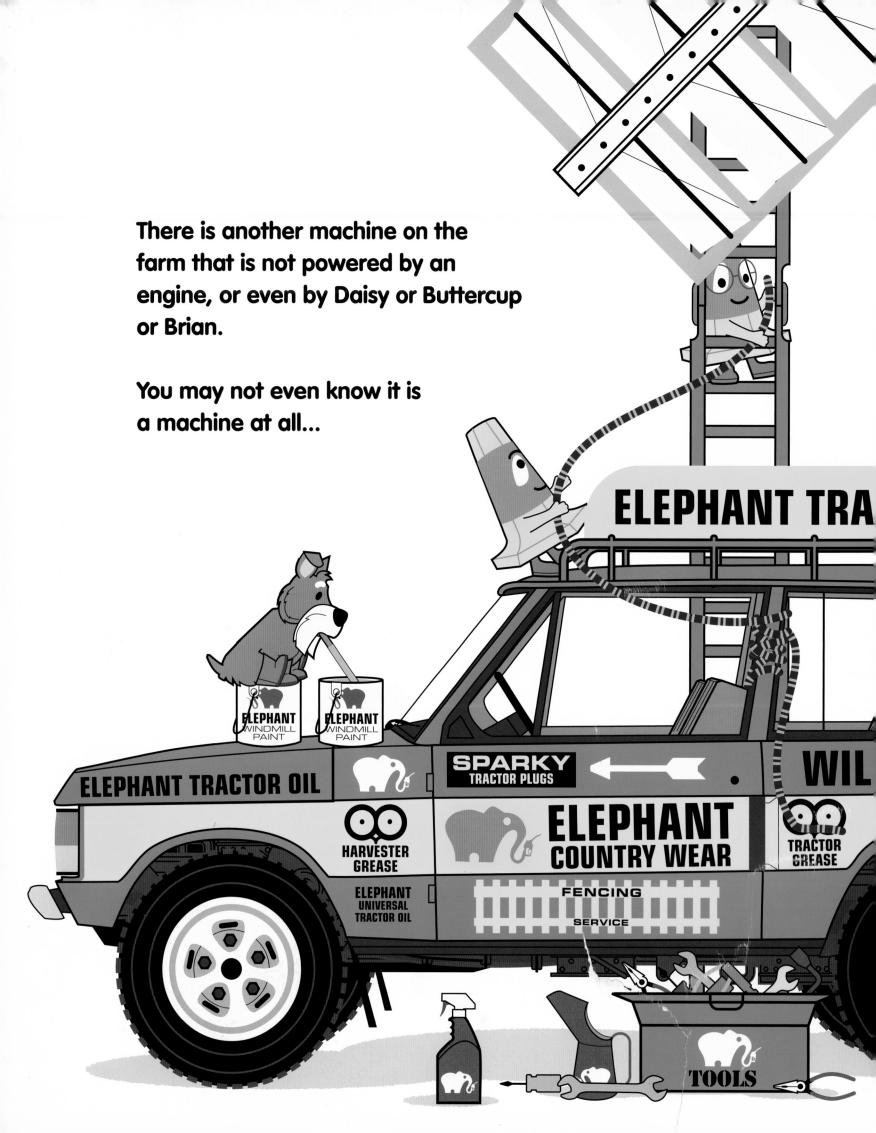

It's a windmill.

It has great big sails which turn in the wind and drive the milling machine inside. This crushes the grain from the wheat until it is flour – which makes bread.

Which reminds me...

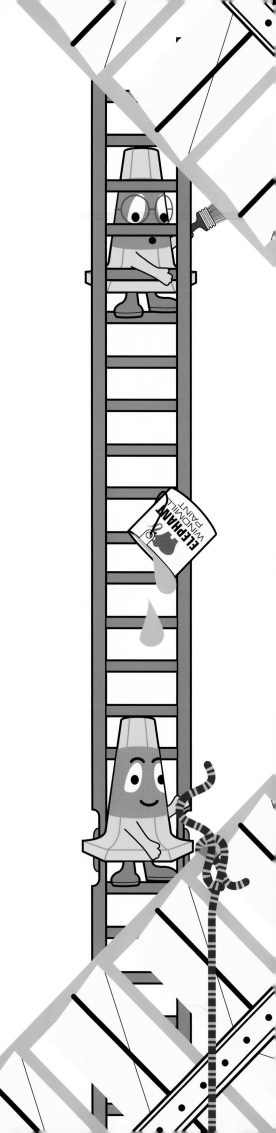

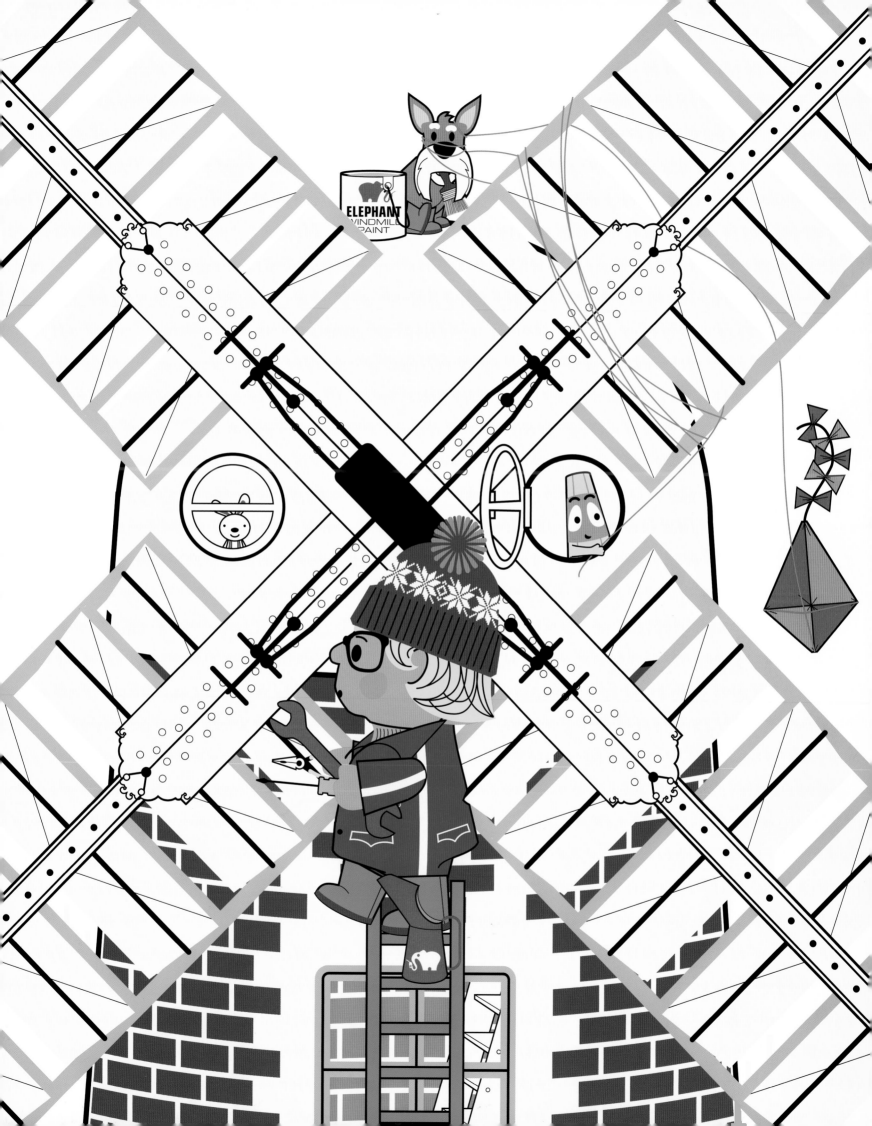

We all got up really early this morning
to show you my tractors –
the one that pulls, and the one that pushes, and the
one that lifts, and the one that scoops (and shakes).

And my farm machines – the steam engine,
and the threshing machine, and the combine
harvester – and of course Daisy and Buttercup
and Brian.

So early that we forgot to have any breakfast!

And farming – and making all that food –
is *very* hungry work!

# More farm machine facts from William Bee

This is how a combine harvester cuts the wheat and separates the grain from the stalks.

Wheat grows in the field.
The top of the wheat is called 'grain' – which is the bit we eat. The rest is straw, which cows and horses sleep on.

The sharp blade – in the green circle – cuts the wheat.
Then big wheels at the front of the combine harvester rotate the wheat onto a conveyor belt (like at a supermarket check out).

Farms grow all sorts of crops other than cereals (like wheat) and vegetables (like potatoes) and fruit (like apples and pears). They also grow flowers (millions of them), mushrooms, nuts, even trees – for Christmas!

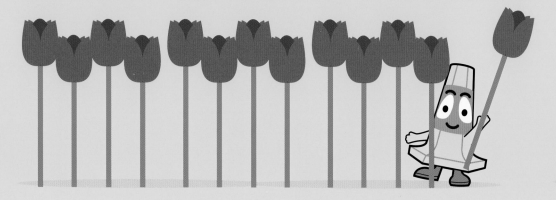

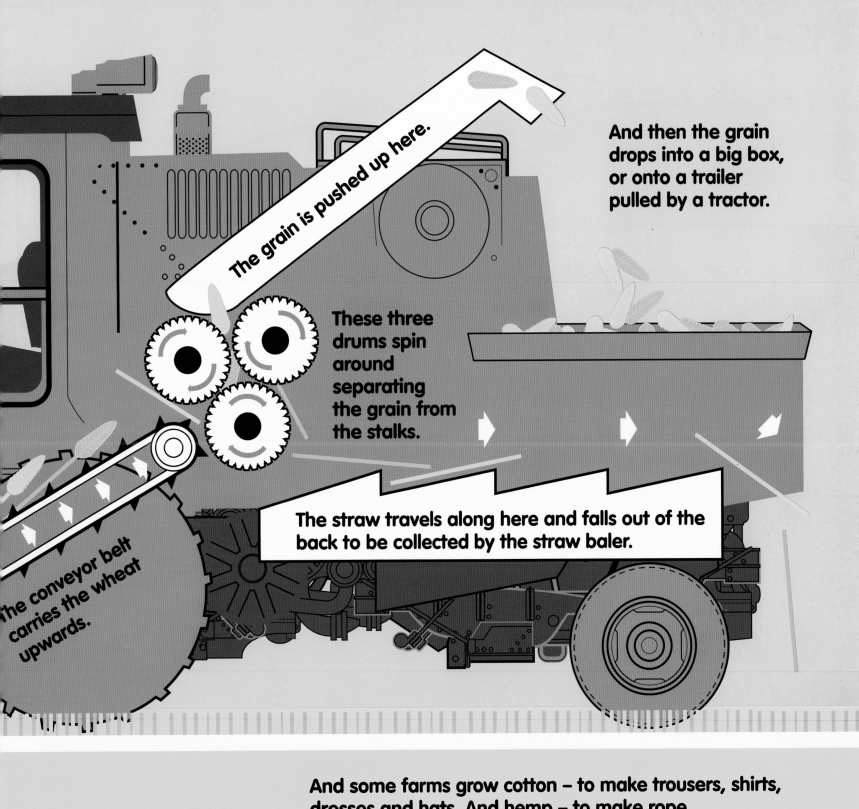

The grain is pushed up here.

And then the grain drops into a big box, or onto a trailer pulled by a tractor.

These three drums spin around separating the grain from the stalks.

The straw travels along here and falls out of the back to be collected by the straw baler.

The conveyor belt carries the wheat upwards.

And some farms grow cotton – to make trousers, shirts, dresses and hats. And hemp – to make rope.
And plants that make medicines and plants that make fuel – even tractor fuel.

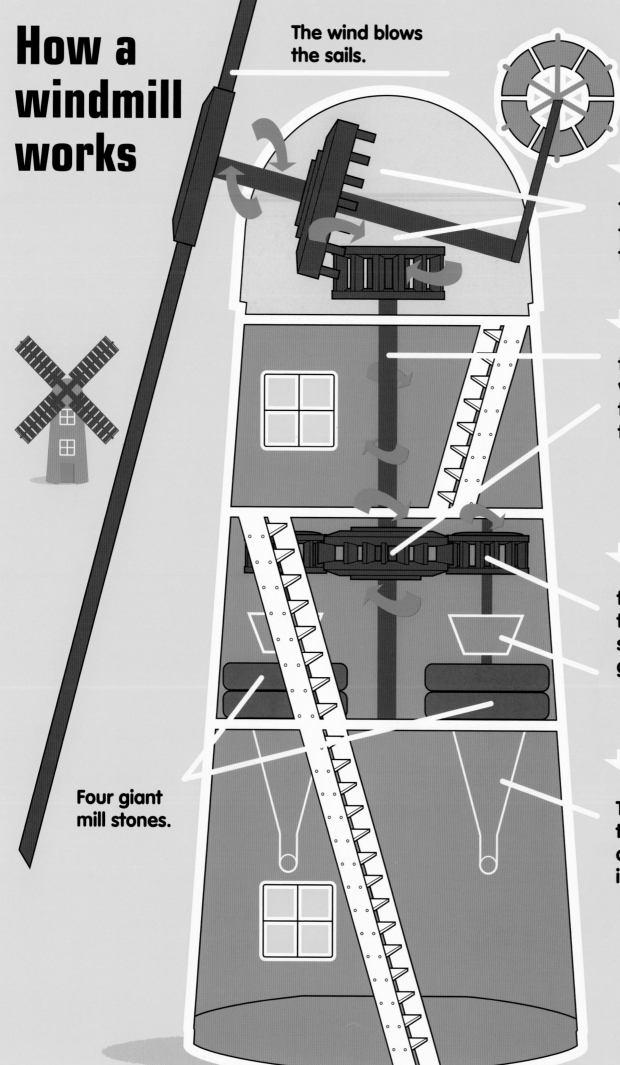

# How a windmill works

**The wind blows the sails.**

**This wheel controls the top of the windmill (in blue) which revolves to turn the sails into the wind.**

**The sails turn these wooden toothed wheels,**

**that turn this wooden shaft, turning another toothed wheel,**

**turning this one that turns the mill stones which crush the grain from this hopper.**

**Four giant mill stones.**

**The grain is crushed by the heavy stones and drops down this chute into a sack.**

# Tractors get bigger and bigger!

As farmers' fields have got larger, and the machines their tractors tow or carry have become more powerful and complex,

so tractors have had to get much bigger, stronger and more powerful.

William Bee's newest tractor (below) is four times as big as his oldest one (at the top).

# They're CRUNCHY!

## WILLIAM BEE'S FARM
### Apple and Pear
### Crunchy Wheat Flakes

750g — 25 Servings

**The Crunchiest Cereal on the Farm!**

ELEPHANT CEREALS

Per portion (30g)

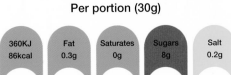

| 360KJ 86kcal | Fat 0.3g | Saturates 0g | Sugars 8g | Salt 0.2g |

Per 100g: 1200KJ / 286kcal

## WILLIAM BEE'S FARM
### Strawberry
### Crunchy Wheat Flakes

750g — 25 Servings

**The Crunchiest Cereal on the Farm!**

ELEPHANT CEREALS

Per portion (30g)

| 366KJ 87.5kcal | Fat 0.3g | Saturates 0g | Sugars 8g | Salt 0.2g |

Per 100g: 1220KJ / 291kcal

## WILLIAM BEE'S FARM
### Blackberry
### Crunchy Wheat Flakes

750g — 25 Servings

**The Crunchiest Cereal on the Farm!**

ELEPHANT CEREALS

Per portion (30g)

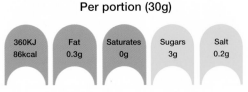

| 360KJ 86kcal | Fat 0.3g | Saturates 0g | Sugars 3g | Salt 0.2g |

Per 100g: 1200KJ / 286kcal

## WILLIAM BEE'S FARM
### Simply Wheat
### Crunchy Wheat Flakes

★★★★

750g — 25 Servings

**The Crunchiest Cereal on the Farm!**

ELEPHANT CEREALS

Per portion (30g)

| 376KJ 90cal | Fat 0.5g | Saturates 0g | Sugars 3g | Salt 0.2g |

Per 100g: 1253KJ / 300kcal

## WILLIAM BEE'S FARM
### Simply Nuts
### Crunchy Wheat Flakes

750g — 25 Servings

**The Crunchiest Cereal on the Farm!**

ELEPHANT CEREALS

Per portion (30g)

| 606KJ 145kcal | Fat 1.5g | Saturates 0.5g | Sugars 4.2g | Salt 0.2g |

Per 100g: 2020KJ / 483kcal

## WILLIAM BEE'S FARM
### Raspberry
### Crunchy Wheat Flakes

750g — 25 Servings

**The Crunchiest Cereal on the Farm!**

ELEPHANT CEREALS

Per portion (30g)

| 389KJ 93kcal | Fat 0.35g | Saturates 0g | Sugars 3g | Salt 0.2g |

Per 100g: 1297KJ / 310kcal

# William Bee's Farm – makers of the VERY BEST breakfast cereals

Available from **ELEPHANT** Service Stations

**ELEPHANT CEREALS**

**If you enjoyed this book, you might also like**
*William Bee's Wonderful World of Trains
and Boats and Planes,* **and**
*William Bee's Wonderful World of Trucks*